Bumble!

Andrew Bickerton

Illustrations by Kevin Smith

Grosvenor House
Publishing Limited

This book is published by
Grosvenor House Publishing Ltd
Link House
140 The Broadway, Tolworth, Surrey, KT6 7HT.
www.grosvenorhousepublishing.co.uk

A CIP record for this book
is available from the British Library

ISBN 978-1-78623-333-2

ACKNOWLEDGEMENTS

My thanks to the pupils of Great Massingham and Harpley primary schools who encouraged me with their positive responses and honest opinions to both of my books and also to Kevin Smith for his impressive Illustrations.

Special thanks also to Friends of the Earth, Buglife and the Bumble Bee Conservation Trust for their expert advice.

Andrew Bickerton 2018.

CONTENTS

Extras:

INTRODUCTION

This is the story of the famous bee named Bumble. I'm sure you must have heard of her and seen her pictures in the newspapers or seen her on television. She has become a household name – a buzzword in fact.

Bumble was a good friend of mine and I loved watching her and her friends busily flying from flower to flower and listening to their buzzing as they gathered the pollen from the blossom on the trees in my garden. They were the heavenly sound of summer!

Well it's been a long time since I saw her; not since after she became famous and then disappeared. So I decided to tell you her story; the story of Bumble's great achievements and rise to fame... and it all begins in a hole in the ground at the bottom of a very old apple tree...

CHAPTER ONE – FIRST DAYS

The early spring sun rose from behind the high garden fence and shone onto the last remaining old apple tree of an orchard. The orchard had been dug out and replaced with part of a large housing estate. All the houses had hard standing for cars at the front and concrete patios and decking at the rear. There were very few flower borders and certainly no space for a vegetable patch.

The warmth of the sun gradually reached a small hole at the base of the apple tree and a drowsy bumblebee slowly emerged and stretched her wings.

"Good morning Bumble!" came a squeaky voice from above. "Where are you going today?"

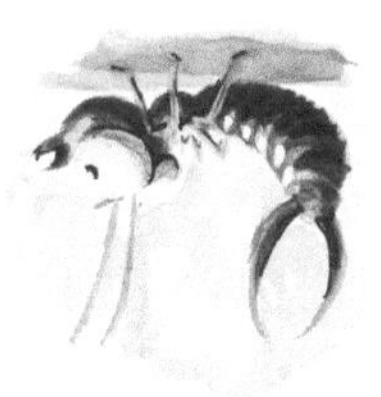

Bumble looked up and saw her friend Eric, an earwig, crawling along the branch overhead.

"Oh, hi there Eric," Bumble replied. "Expect I'll be foraging again over by them allotments. Got to get loads of nectar for her majesty to give her all the energy wot she needs."

"Oh Bumble, your grammar is getting worse," said Eric, who was a very particular earwig and always precise in his actions and speech. "You really ought to get some lessons you know."

"I ain't got time for lessons, Eric. I can't hang around here like you all day. I've got work to do," and with a loud buzz Bumble flew off to start her day's work.

She had not flown very far when she met Wayne. Wayne was a wasp and the local tearaway. Wayne loved to fly around annoying all the local residents.

"Watch'ya Bumble," said Wayne. "Coming for a bit of fun?"

"Where are you going, Wayne?" Bumble asked.

"I'm off to find some kids with cans of drink," Wayne sniggered. "I don't half laugh when I buzz round 'em and make 'em drop their cans and watch 'em run away screaming. I then gets to drink some of what they leave. Ha! Ha! Are you coming?"

"No. I've got important work to do. The Queen and her larvae need feeding as quick as possible. I can't play around all day like you," Bumble said and left Wayne hovering behind her.

After a few minutes Bumble arrived at the allotments. "These should have plenty of flowers," she said to herself and flew over to the vegetable plots...

What vegetable plots! They had all been dug up and huge machines were shaking the ground all around. Dust clouds blinded her and fumes from their engines began to choke her.

Confused and shaken Bumble managed to fly to what was left of a hedge at the end of the allotments. There she found Holly, a small blue butterfly, shaking with fear and sobbing into her wings.

"Holly! It's me, your friend, Bumble. Stop crying and follow me out of here," murmured Bumble soothingly.

"Oh Bumble! It's horrible!" cried Holly. "I'm so scared of those gigantic monsters. Will they destroy everything?"

"I don't know, Holly, but we must get out of here right now. One of them things is coming towards us! Quick! Follow me!"

Bumble flew over the hedge with Holly fluttering behind her. The huge digger grabbed the hedge and tore it out of the earth.

It then swung round and dumped it into a truck, which was already half full of shrubs and small trees ready to put on the bonfire smouldering nearby.

"Phew! That was close Holly," Bumble said. "We might have ended up on that bonfire."

“That was my home,” Holly sobbed. “I can’t bear to watch. Let’s get away from here, please, Bumble.”

“Ok,” Bumble agreed. “We’ll fly over to that garden. There’s bound to be some flowers for us there.”

A high new fence surrounded the garden and once they had flown over it Bumble and Holly settled in a flower border, safe from all the dangers.

They rested for a short while and then began searching for flowers to feed from. But this was early spring and very few flowers were open. Those that were open provided very little pollen or nectar. The new garden was almost empty except for a large patio and newly laid lawn.

“This doesn’t look very promising,” mumbled Bumble. “I’ll go over to that patch of grass. There might be some clover or some dandelions for me.”

“I can see some ivy on that tree,” said Holly. “That might be somewhere for me to lay my eggs. I don’t know what I’d have done if you hadn’t come along.”

“It was nothing,” Bumble replied trying not to show her pride. “I’ll see you around.”

Bumble flew over to the patch of grass but finding very little clover or any dandelions she made her way back home. The little bit of nectar and few grains of pollen were not much to show for a morning’s work and certainly not enough to satisfy all the larvae. Feeling very disheartened Bumble made her way back to the apple tree where her Queen would be waiting anxiously for her.

CHAPTER TWO – FURTHER AFIELD

As she settled at the bottom of the familiar trunk Eric's squeaky voice made her look up.

"Hello Bumble," Eric called. "Did you have a good forage this morning?"

"Can't stop now, Eric," Bumble replied, "I've got to deliver food to the Queen. She's starving." And with that Bumble quickly crawled into the hole that led to the nest housing the Queen.

When Bumble finally reached the Queen she explained what had happened and emptied her baskets of what little pollen she had managed to collect. The Queen looked very disappointed.

"Oh, Bumble," she sighed, "we won't survive if you can't do better than this. All my other workers have returned and nearly every one with the same sad story. Now is the most important time for us. Without proper food our colony will die and we will have no future. Please go out again, Bumble. You will have to fly further afield."

"Right, Your Majesty," said Bumble trying to sound confident. "I won't let you all die, I promise."

"Thank you Bumble. I know I can depend on you!"

Bumble scrambled back to the entrance with the Queen's last words ringing in her head, ***"I know I can depend on you."***

Eric watched his friend stagger out of the hole and knew something was bothering her. "What's wrong?" he asked. "Is the Queen angry with you?"

"No. It's worse than that!" she replied. "If I can't collect more food the colony may die. She is depending on me. What can I do?"

"Well," said Eric after a few moments, "You will just have to fly further afield."

"That's what she told me, further afield... a field! That's it! I need to find a field full of flowers."

"A fat chance of that!" said a voice.

It was Basil. Basil was a shield bug and Basil always looked on the gloomy side of things. "The farmers kill all the wild flowers and they will kill you as well if you don't look out!"

"They wouldn't kill me," Bumble replied. "I'm their friend."

"They wouldn't mean to but they will, mark my words," warned Basil.

"You're too... too... pesimessitistic," stammered Bumble.

"I think you mean pessimistic," corrected Eric. "It means you always look on the bad side of things, Basil."

“I’ve yet to see the good side of things. Things always start off bad and end up worse,” Basil muttered.

Suddenly Basil was knocked off his leaf by a whizzing wasp.

“Look on the other side then you old misery. There’s plenty of fun to be had if you look for it!” laughed Wayne.

“So what’s the problem Bumble?” asked Wayne. “Can I help?”

As Basil was struggling back onto his six feet and grumbling about life in general, Bumble explained to Wayne, with frequent corrections from Eric, all that had happened and how she would have to fly further afield in search of food for the Queen.

“That sounds like a bit of an adventure to me!” said Wayne. “What are we all waiting for?”

“Well I’m not feeling up to any adventures after being buffeted by a buffoon!” grumbled Basil.

“I try to avoid too much excitement, Wayne. I like to take things steady,” Eric explained as he crawled into a crack in the bark.

“Bumble? What about you? We won’t get anywhere sitting about here and moaning. We need to start searching right away!” Wayne said. He had never sounded this serious before.

“You’re right, Wayne. Two of us stand more chance than one so let’s go!” Bumble began to feel better now that she had someone to help her. She shouted goodbye to Eric and Basil and set off with her new friend to see if they could find flowers, ‘further afield’.

"No good will come of this, you mark my words," warned Basil who had finally managed to climb back onto the leaf where he had been sitting before being so rudely disturbed.

As they were flying along Wayne told Bumble about all the fun he had had that morning annoying people and how he was looking forward to the summer when people would be having picnics with jam and drinks and other delicious food to taste. Usually Bumble would have found Wayne's excited chatter very annoying but now she found it comforting and amusing.

They eventually arrived at a field but it had been ploughed ready for a new crop and the verges were weed free and flower free. The next field had a crop of winter barley growing. It looked very healthy, a sea of bright green but yet again they could find no flowers to feed on.

"We have flown all this way for nothing," Bumble said sadly. "Perhaps we should give up and go home."

"Let's try one more field. Come on, through that gap over there," encouraged Wayne as he started to fly towards it. Bumble followed slowly and by the time she had reached the gap in the hedge she could hear Wayne shouting excitedly. "Wow! Come and see what I've found! It's fantastic!"

Bumble flew through the gap and couldn't believe her eyes – a whole field full of bright yellow flowers in bloom and their deliciously sweet scent drifted over her.

"This is brilliant! It's just what we need!" exclaimed Bumble and she did a victory roll to celebrate. "I must get back and give the good news to the Queen."

"And I'll zoom round to Zippy and the rest of the hoverfly gang. They won't believe it when I tell them. Reckon they might treat me with more respect from now on," said Wayne, feeling rather proud of himself.

"Ok, Wayne," replied Bumble. "We have got to let everyone know."

The two excited and happy friends flew as fast as they could to spread the good news. In her excitement, Bumble had forgotten to collect any nectar or pollen but she felt certain she would soon be collecting plenty for everyone.

CHAPTER THREE – DISASTER!

When Bumble arrived at her apple tree Eric and Basil were waiting for her.

"How did it go?" asked Eric.

"Badly, I expect," sighed Basil.

"Great!" replied Bumble. "We found a whole field of flowers. I can't stop – gotta tell the Queen the good news."

And with that she disappeared into the nest.

"What do you say to that, Basil?" asked Eric, smiling.

"It will turn out badly, wait and see," Basil replied as he climbed onto another leaf. "It always does!"

In the nest Bumble excitedly told the Queen about the great discovery.

"Well done, Bumble. Well done! You've saved all our lives," she said.

"It wasn't me who found the field, Your Majesty. It was Wayne. He found it when I had about given up," Bumble said.

"Congratulate him for me please and show all our workers where this field is so they can get foraging while the weather is so good."

"Certainly, Your Majesty and I will spread the good news to our hoverfly friends as well as those early butterflies who are out and about."

Bumble crawled from the dark chamber into beautiful spring sunshine. All around her leaves were emerging and the birds were busily building nests and singing. It had been a long and tiring day but now she was full of new energy and she began to tell all her workmates about the field and issued directions where to find it.

In no time at all swarms of insects including butterflies, beetles and other bugs were heading for Bumble's field. Wayne had also got a gang together to join in the feast.

When Bumble arrived the golden field was alive with every kind of insect happily feeding and pollinating the crop. The sun was shining and a gentle breeze blew the sweet scent of the oil seed across the field. Everything seemed perfect...

"Hi Bumble. Thanks so much for telling us," said Holly as she fluttered happily towards her.

"This is really great, Bumble!" shouted Zippy, the hoverfly, as she settled briefly on a flower and then flew backwards to the next bloom. She always was a show-off!

Bumble looked around and was pleased to see so many of her workmates busily collecting the nectar and pollen. She soon found a plant full of the precious food and got to work. She was so engrossed in filling her empty pockets she did not hear the sound of an approaching machine.

It got closer...

and closer...

and closer...

until Bumble felt the vibrations shaking through her feet.

She flew up and turned around. What she saw was a gigantic metal bug with long outstretched arms bearing down on her.

Then she noticed that a cloud of rain was coming from those long arms and soaking all the flowers. As she watched bees, hoverflies, beetles and other bugs began falling from the flowers and dropping lifeless onto the ground!

She tried to warn everybody but her cries were drowned out by the rumbling and roaring coming from the machine.

"Look out Bumble! I'll stop that beast!" shouted Wayne, and Bumble watched as her brave friend flew straight at the monster. That was the last Bumble saw of him as he disappeared in a cloud of dust and spray.

Bumble was horrified and very, very frightened. Worst of all – she felt that she was to blame!

Slowly she made her way back home wondering how she was going to tell the Queen about the disaster that had happened. How would they ever recover from this? She approached the apple tree where the Queen was waiting and there were Eric and Basil.

Eric could see that all was not well. "What has happened? Where is everybody?" he asked.

"It's dreadful, a disaster! We're finished!" Bumble sobbed and she proceeded to tell them all that had occurred,

"That's terrible!" Eric said. "What will you do?"

"I don't know," she replied. "That field was our last hope."

"It could have been worse," Basil said. "It usually is and probably will be."

"You're right," Bumble agreed as she made her way down to tell the Queen.

Somehow Bumble managed to give the Queen the terrible news and, after a little while, she crawled back to the open. There, to her surprise, was Wayne. He was covered in goo and looked exhausted.

"Oh Wayne, you're back!" exclaimed Bumble.

"Worse luck!" muttered Basil.

"I thought you were a goner," Bumble said. "How did you manage to escape?"

"I got inside the cabin and kept buzzing the driver. He had to stop and so I scarpered," Wayne replied.

"What about the rest? Did anyone else survive?"

"I reckon so, although I only just got away meself," Wayne said.

"That should be 'myself', Wayne," corrected Eric who had been listening quietly. "Your grammar is as bad as Bumble's."

"I ain't got a grandma so don't insult her," Wayne replied angrily.

Just then two tattered and battered butterflies approached them. As they got nearer Bumble recognised Holly, the blue butterfly she had rescued at the allotments. With her was a large, impressive butterfly with black, red and white wings. He was a red Admiral and usually very impressive in his uniform but now his wings were dull and dusty and he looked very much the worse for wear.

"Mind if we rest a while? We're rather exhausted," sighed the Admiral.

"I feel very, very tired," said Holly and promptly fell asleep on a nettle.

"How many more casualties are there, Admiral?" asked Basil, who was rather impressed by him.

"Hundreds! It's like a battlefield. Bodies everywhere and the wounded are crawling and fluttering feebly on the ground. Never seen anything like it in all me life!" the Admiral replied sadly.

"We've got to do something. We can't go on being killed by these spraying monsters," Eric said.

"But what can we do?" Bumble asked. "We can't fight those things. We're too small to stop them."

"I could get the gang, or what's left of 'em. They're real fighters they are. We'd show 'em!" Wayne said and buzzed Basil and Eric making them both fall off their perches.

"Save your energy," Bumble said. "A few wasps aren't going to make any difference."

CHAPTER FOUR – HOLLY'S GREAT IDEA

"What we need is a campaign," said the Admiral. "You have to have a campaign. That's what is needed."

There followed a few seconds of silence when everybody gave this idea some thought. The problem was that Holly was still sound asleep, Basil didn't know what was meant by 'a campaign', Wayne was still feeling ready for a fight and Eric was involved in climbing back into the tree.

At last Bumble asked the Admiral what sort of campaign did he think might work.

The Admiral was not too sure but didn't want to show it so he said, "Well, a campaign that puts a stop to all this killing of us insects; gets people to change what they're doing. That sort of thing."

"You mean we should try to persuade them to stop spraying us?"

"And killing all the flowers," said Holly, who had just woken up. "We need flowers. Grass isn't much use to us."

"That's right, Holly, **we need flowers and flowers need us**!" Bumble said.

"Absolutely, couldn't have put it better meself, Bumble," the Admiral declared.

"And how do you think you're going to get them to listen to you?" asked Basil.

"We could all shout together. They might listen then," suggested Eric.

"Don't make me laugh!" Wayne said. "If we all made as much noise as we could they'd never hear us above the row they make all the time."

"And anyway they've all started going around with plugs and wires in their ears," Holly added.

"They don't see anything around them either anymore. They spend all the time looking at those things in their hands," Bumble said. "It's impossible!"

"What are they listening to?" the Admiral asked.

"Some sort of music, I reckon," Wayne replied. "Mostly songs, I've heard."

"Well that's what we must do, make a song that they will listen to," the Admiral said.

"None of us can sing," Basil pointed out.

"I can buzz loudly," said Wayne, "especially when I get angry!"

"The only song is my buzzing with my wings," Bumble said. "But I can do a kind of rapping."

"What's rapping?" asked Eric.

"Some sort of paper I think," suggested Basil.

"Woodpeckers do a lot of rapping. Extremely noisy they are," said the Admiral.

"No. I mean a kind of song."

"Let's hear it then," Wayne said.

"Yes, come on Bumble," said Holly.

"Come on Bumble," they all pleaded and eventually Bumble sang them a rap song that she had been composing in her head as she foraged.

They were all very impressed. Eric pointed out some grammar mistakes and Basil said that he thought it wasn't actually singing like the thrushes and blackbirds but even he applauded enthusiastically. There then followed various ideas about how Bumble's song could be improved, not all of them welcome.

A lot of suggestions were made about how they could get this song heard: such as busking on the streets, getting all the bees, wasps and hoverflies to sing it together and teaching the birds to twitter it, but none of them sounded very convincing. Their initial enthusiasm slowly sank into a gloomy silence...

And then Holly said, **"You could enter a talent show!"**

"A talent show! That's it – a talent show! Brilliant!" exclaimed Basil. He had never sounded so excited.

"You would have to have an audition but I'm sure you'd get accepted and then lots of people would hear you, especially if it was on television," said Holly. Everybody agreed, including Basil, that it was **a really good idea**.

The Admiral opened his bright wings and announced, "Well done team. We have now got a campaign plan. Bumble will enter a talent show with her song, with our support, of course. But first

Bumble you must get permission from the Queen and then you will need to follow a strict routine of practice and rest so you can be at your very best come the audition."

It was agreed to let all the other insects know of the plan and to find where and when the next auditions for a television talent show would take place. As it was now growing dark the first moths appeared and they too were told of the dreadful events of the day and the plan involving Bumble's song.

The first stars began to appear as the friends said goodnight to one another and made their way home for a night's rest. Bumble spent a very restless night with her head full of the events of that dreadful day and feeling nervous about a possible audition for a television talent show. So much now depended on her!

CHAPTER FIVE – BUMBLE'S GOT TALENT

The day for the talent show auditions arrived. It was to be held in a local school hall where various acts were already assembled. They were astonished to see Bumble and her friends and couldn't believe that a bumblebee had any chance at all. Many of them tried to frighten Bumble away but Wayne and his friends arrived and within a few minutes only two acts remained, the rest having disappeared down the street followed by a swarm of angry wasps.

A door opened and a man shouted, "Next! The Buzzword Rap singer, please." He looked around to see who might come forward but nobody moved.

"Where is everybody?" he asked.

"They've all gone home," said Bumble. "I'm the Buzzword Rap singer, sir."

"YOU!" exclaimed the man. "But you're just a common bumblebee. Is this a joke?"

"No joke," the Admiral replied. "We're very serious and Bumble is very good. You'll see."

"Oh no, sorry, but we don't want any bees on the show. We have enough problems with the dogs and the cats without bees flying about as well."

"Oh please give her a chance," pleaded Holly. "I know you'll change your mind once you've heard her song."

"Oh, all right," he said. "But you lot wait outside."

They all did as they were asked and Bumble nervously followed the man through the door to the school hall to begin her audition. This was her big moment; so much depended on her song.

As she looked around the hall she saw rows of children who had come to watch. They looked at her in astonishment and some even began to giggle at the sight of a bumblebee about to perform in a talent show.

"Do you want any music?" the producer asked.

"N... n... no th... th... thank you," Bumble stammered. "I m... m... make my own."

"Right, let's get on with it then," he said. And Bumble began her performance.

"Now I is a bee

A simple bumblebee

I come from a tree

Near a big city..."

Five minutes later Bumble emerged from the school hall and her friends could tell that things had gone badly.

"What happened?" Wayne asked.

"Didn't they like your song?" asked Holly.

"Well, I was very nervous and kept forgetting the words to start with, but eventually I finished it. Some of the children liked it, I think, but the producer didn't and so I won't be performing in the show. I'm sorry everybody. I'm really sorry," said Bumble.

"It's not your fault," said the Admiral. "You did your best."

"Do you want me to go in there?" asked Wayne who was beginning to get angry again.

"No, no. It wouldn't change anything and you would only scare the children," Bumble replied. "I just want to go home."

"We'll just have to think of something else," said the Admiral as the group made their way back home. "I'll get my thinking cap on. I'm sure something will turn up!"

The others were not so sure. If they couldn't get people to listen to them what hope was there?

When Bumble arrived back home Eric and Basil were waiting for her eager to hear how things went but, when they saw her, they knew. They watched Bumble settle slowly onto the ground and crawl into the entrance of the nest.

Basil said, "Oh well, just as I thought. It was a stupid idea. Things will only get worse, Eric. They always do!"

Eric felt that, for once, Basil was right.

CHAPTER SIX – BUMBLE GOES VIRAL!

A few weeks later, when spring had made way for early summer, Bumble and the other workers were foraging in some bee-friendly gardens when Wayne flew excitedly up to her.

"Bumble! Bumble! Have you heard?" he asked. "They're playing your song. They're playing your song!"

"Who are Wayne?" she asked.

"Everyone! Everybody's listening to your performance in that school hall! You've gone viral!" he exclaimed.

"Calm down," Bumble said, "and explain what it is you're making so much fuss about."

"I don't know how it happened but they've got you singing on those ear things they're listening to all the time. I heard them chatting about it in the playground. They reckon you've gone viral!"

"I don't like the sound of that Wayne. I don't have a virus and I don't want one."

"I don't think it's a bad virus, Bumble. It's not a disease."

"This doesn't make sense. You're imagining things Wayne. I've got to get on with my work," she said and began foraging again.

Just then a girl came into the garden. She was wearing headphones and skipping from side to side as she approached the flower bed. A small boy holding a football followed her.

"What're you listening to Sis?" he shouted.

"The song by that bumblebee I recorded," she replied. "Everybody's gone mad about it. They're watching it on YouTube and Facebook and everything. I've had thousands of hits already."

"Can I listen to it? Can I?" he pleaded.

"Yes, okay Freddie," she replied and taking the wires out of her ears she turned up the volume on her phone. It was definitely Bumble singing. It was definitely Bumble's song!

"That's great!" Freddie exclaimed. "You're famous now. Will you be on the telly, Daisy?"

"It's not me who should be on the television. It's the bee who sang the song. We've got to find her so she knows about it, Freddie. Will you help?"

"Okay. What does she look like?"

"Well... I looked her up on a bee identification web site. She is the early bumblebee with two yellow stripes and an orange tail. Look."

The girl showed her brother a picture of a bee on her phone.

"She looks exactly like **this** bee," replied Freddie, pointing at Bumble who was sitting very still in the middle of a flower.

Daisy bent down and compared the picture on her phone with Bumble. "Are you the bee who sang this song?" she asked.

Bumble was too dumbstruck to reply. There was so much to take in and she could not believe this was actually happening.

The girl crouched down closer to Bumble and said, "You are. I **know** you are. I would recognise you anywhere! Freddie, this is the bee. We've found her! We've found her!"

"Hurrah!" shouted Freddie and kicked the football into the air which nearly landed on Wayne who was busy collecting material for nest building.

The children danced around the garden playing Bumble's song and after a little while Bumble found herself joining in with them. When they stopped for a rest, Daisy told Bumble that she had filmed her performance at the audition on her phone and sent it to her friends. They had loved it and sent it on to other children and so on and so on until the whole country was talking about it. It had even been played on the radio. Everybody knew about Bumble's song.

"But do they understand it?" Bumble asked. "It's not just a song it's much more important than that."

“I think most people understand,” said Daisy. “Well I do anyway. We have to stop killing the bees.”

“Or we won’t get any fruit!” Freddie said. “And I like apples, and pears, and strawberries, and...”

“It’s not just us bees, you know, it’s all of the other pollinators as well,” said Bumble.

“And that includes me!” shouted Wayne as he buzzed around them. “I also eat a lot of pests, I do! Us wasps do a lot of good you know.”

“Don’t mind him,” said Bumble when she saw the children trying to dodge him. “His buzz is worse than his sting. In fact,” she whispered, “being a male wasp, he can’t sting at all!”

Then Daisy took a photo of Bumble on her phone to send to all her Facebook friends, saying that now she had found her, everybody would want to meet her and hear her sing again. Just then a woman came out of the house and called the children in for their tea and they both ran to her, eager to tell their mother all about meeting Bumble in the garden.

Wayne turned to Bumble and said, “Now do you believe me? Your song is famous and so are you!”

“I’m not sure I want that, Wayne. I just want everybody to stop killing us and to make sure that there is food for everybody, including us,” and Bumble turned for home again with a million thoughts buzzing around in her head.

CHAPTER SEVEN – BUMBLE IS A 'CELEB'

The next few weeks were completely crazy. Bumble's song was made into a record and immediately went to number one with all the money going to bumblebee protection. There were lots of interviews with Bumble on radio and television where she described the problems she and other pollinators had faced and the terrible day when so many of her friends died. Newspapers had headlines such as 'SAVE OUR BEES!' and 'BUMBLE'S A STAR!'

She made guest appearances on *'The X Factor'* as well as *'Strictly Come Dancing'* but not on her own. Accompanying her were some other bees as well as Wayne and his mates who were particularly good at doing the funky moves.

People started wearing T-shirts with 'Save Our Bees' on the front. Chain stores promoted the campaign with 'Bee Happy' shopping bags and many garden centres sold out of bee-friendly plants.

One refuse company even painted pictures of Bumble on their lorries and councils began sowing wild flowers on roadsides and in their parks.

Pop groups staged special concerts in aid of pollinators and Bumble was asked to appear on the Pyramid Stage at Glastonbury. The BBC launched a brand new show called *'The Great British Buzz-Off'* which became so popular that all the 'celebs' wanted to appear on it.

The campaign grew and grew. Laws were passed and all the dangerous pesticides were banned. More and more farmers began growing wild flowers on the edges of fields and more people began to change their gardens to make them a home for nature including insects, birds and all wildlife. Bumble became a national hero and was even awarded an O.Bee.E!

Now that the future for bees, hoverflies, butterflies and other flying insects looked much brighter Bumble felt that her work was done. This life of a celebrity was definitely not for her. She was a worker bee and she was never happier than when she was foraging collecting nectar for all her family. She decided to return to her home, to her life with her old friends, to the old apple tree where she was born and began her great adventure.

CHAPTER EIGHT – DREAMS

She knew the way to her home but it seemed much further than she remembered and she often had to stop and rest before she could carry on. After what seemed like many more miles Bumble was too exhausted to continue. She dropped onto a verge and crawled towards the hedge. There she found a warm sheltered spot amongst some ivy and fell into a deep, deep sleep...

*****

She woke to find herself in a beautiful wildflower meadow. Everywhere Bumble looked colourful flowers were swaying gently in the breeze: poppies, cornflowers, corn marigolds, knapweeds, primroses, cowslips; so many different flowers from different seasons, all flowering at the same time!

And Bumble could hear the songs of countless birds coming from the surrounding trees: blackbirds, song thrushes, robins, nightingales and in the bright blue sky above her skylarks and swallows singing and twittering joyfully. She stretched her wings and flew towards the nearby patch of oxeye daisies to begin gathering pollen and sip the sweet nectar. There were already many nectar feeding insects there. In fact the whole meadow was alive with butterflies, bees and every kind of insect happily feeding on the flowers.

As Bumble approached she thought she could recognise some of the butterflies and bees. Surely she must be mistaken! They couldn't possibly be her old friends; her friends who had followed her to that field on that fateful day; her friends who had been poisoned by the insecticide; her friends who had died.

"Hi Bumble! Is that you?" a hoverfly shouted. "Have you just arrived?"

"Err, yes," replied Bumble. "Zippy! What are you doing here?"

"Hey everybody!" shouted Zippy. "Look who's here! It's Bumble. Bumble's come and joined us!"

"Bumble! Bumble! It's Bumble!" shouted everybody. "Hurrah for Bumble!"

All the insects, bees, butterflies, hoverflies, moths, beetles and wasps came flying over to greet her.

"This can't be... be... happening," stammered the confused Bumble. "Reckon I must be 'aving one of me dreams."

"One of **my** dreams you mean," came a familiar voice.

Bumble looked down and saw her best friend Eric who was crawling up the stem of a daisy.

"Eric! Is that you? What are you doing here?" gasped Bumble.

"The same as you, dear Bumble, having a wonderful time."

"Wow!" exclaimed the astonished Bumble. "It's heaven here, isn't it."

"Yes," replied everybody. "You're absolutely right. **This is heaven**!"

****

Gradually Bumble opened her eyes. She was still in the warm hedge and she realised that she **had been dreaming** after all! But, although it was only a dream, she also knew that dreams **can** come true and her dream was a lot closer to coming true now that everybody was joining her campaign.

With the dream still alive in her head she set off for home, a happy bee, a bee full of hope, looking forward to continuing her work amongst the blossom and flowers in a heavenly new bee-friendly world.

THE END

THE BUZZWORD RAP

Now I is a bee

A simple humble bee

I come from a tree

Near a big city.

Searching for some flowers

For hours and hours

I'm just as busy

As a bee can be.

Yes I'm as busy

As a bee can be.

But things is getting' bad

It makes me real sad.

I'm losin' all me friends

That I once had.

Summat is wrong,

I don't know what.

The flowers have gone

This here song is all I've got.

Need all of you to help

To stop the rot.

So come on everyone

Let's start a campaign

To stop what they're doin'

Causing all this pain.

Make 'em listen

Make 'em listen

Do the social media stuff

Facebook and the like

March in the streets

Or protest on your bike.

'Cos if we don't stop the sprayin'

This is what I'm sayin'

We'll be looking at the end

Of every pollinating friend

Of the flowers and the fruit

On which you all depend.

This is what I'm sayin'

If we don't stop the sprayin'

We'll be looking at the end

Of every pollinating friend

Of the flowers and the fruit

On which you all depend.

Got it?

WHAT DO YOU KNOW ABOUT POLLINATORS?

- Bumblebees, honeybees, hoverflies, butterflies, moths, wasps and many more flying insects are pollinators.
- Pollinators move from flower to flower collecting nectar to feed on. By doing this they also pass pollen between the plants, which plants need to reproduce.
- Many types of fruit and vegetables such as beans, peas, apples raspberries and strawberries are produced on plants that have to be pollinated to produce good quality yields.
- There are over 250 types of wild bee in the UK but 35 species are at risk of dying out. Thirteen types of wild bees are already extinct.
- Adult bees feed on nectar and feed their young with pollen.
- There has been a loss of over 97% of wild flower meadows in the last 100 years. This is a major cause of the decline of many of our pollinators.
- Intensive farming with the use of herbicides to control weeds and pesticides to control pests can also harm bees and other pollinators.
- The over use of chemicals, strimmers and lawnmowers in our gardens results in an unfriendly environment for all wildlife.
- We need pollinators for over a third of the food we eat.
- Pollinators are worth £691 million a year to the UK alone.
- Low maintenance gardens with patios, decking and concrete for off-road parking have replaced hedges, flower borders and vegetable plots.
- Housing estates, new roads and other developments have reduced our natural spaces.
- In fact male wasps do not have a sting and only emerge in late summer.
- Farmers do not spray pesticides on flowering crops but the seed of oil seed rape is coated with a chemical which is harmful to pollinating insects.

HOW YOU CAN HELP

- Join Bumble's campaign!
- Learn *"The Buzzword Rap".* Get your friends to perform it with you!
- Learn to identify the types of pollinators. Take pictures and upload them to the ispot website: https://www.opalexplorenature.org/ispot
- Buy or make a bug/bee hotel.
- Make your garden more bee friendly.
- Make your school more bee friendly!
- Look on the web for ideas and advice. Visit_the web sites of Friends of the Earth, The Bumbebee Conservation Trust and Buglife.
- Share this book with your friends.
- Go to your local garden centre and select bee friendly seeds for beds and pots.
- Get your parents involved. Use your powers of persuasion on them!
- Visit your local park and see if they are bee friendly.
- Visit nature reserves and find out more.
- Write your own story about a pollinator or make up your own poem about bees or moths or butterflies.
- Get outside and enjoy the wonderful world of nature.

ABOUT THE AUTHOR

Andrew Bickerton is a retired English teacher who lives in a small village in Norfolk England. He has written and directed many amateur dramatic productions and published one other children's book for younger children entitled "LEAF".

"Bumble!" continues his concern for the future of our natural environment and its wildlife.

Lightning Source UK Ltd.
Milton Keynes UK
UKHW050908071119
353046UK00001B/13/P
* 9 7 8 1 7 8 6 2 3 3 3 3 2 *